Missing

{ by M. Sobel Spirn
illustrated by Niamh O'Connor }

Librarian Reviewer
Marci Peschke
Librarian, Dallas Independent School District
MA Education Reading Specialist, Stephen F. Austin State University
Learning Resources Endorsement, Texas Women's University

Reading Consultant
Mark DeYoung
Classroom Teacher, Edina Public Schools, MN
BA in Elementary Education, Central College
MS in Curriculum & Instruction, University of MN

STONE ARCH BOOKS
Minneapolis San Diego

Vortex Books are published by Stone Arch Books,
151 Good Counsel Drive, P.O. Box 669,
Mankato, Minnesota 56002.
www.stonearchbooks.com

Library of Congress Cataloging-in-Publication Data
Spirn, Michele.

  Missing / by M. Sobel Spirn; illustrated by Niamh O'Connor.
  p. cm. — (Vortex Books)
  Summary: Eleven-year-old Sam lies so often that when his father
is kidnapped, no one believes him, so Sam and his best friend Josh try to
solve the crime themselves.
  ISBN-13: 978-1-59889-067-9 (hardcover)
  ISBN-10: 1-59889-067-0 (hardcover)
  ISBN-13: 978-1-59889-278-9 (paperback)
  ISBN-10: 1-59889-278-9 (paperback)
  [1. Honesty—Fiction. 2. Kidnapping—Fiction.] I. O'Connor, Niamh,
ill. II. Title. III. Series.
  PZ7.S757Mi 2007
  [Fic]—dc22   2006007680

Art Director: Heather Kindseth
Graphic Designer: Kay Fraser

Photo Credits
Karon Dubke, cover images

1 2 3 4 5 6 11 10 09 08 07 06

Printed in the United States of America.

{ Table of Contents }

Chapter 1

Earthquake Stories

"Where's your math homework?" Mrs. Carter stood over Sam and glared at him. The rest of the class watched. What excuse would Sam come up with this time?

Sam looked up at his teacher. "There was a problem, Mrs. Carter," he said.

"There always is," she answered.

"No, really, this time it isn't my fault. We were in California for vacation. There was an earthquake. My homework got swallowed up," Sam said, looking up at his teacher with pleading eyes.

"Really? I didn't hear about any earthquake. It wasn't on the news," Mrs. Carter said.

"You probably missed it. It wasn't a very big one," Sam said.

"Just big enough to eat your homework," Mrs. Carter said. Some students laughed. They stopped quickly when Mrs. Carter turned around.

"I'd better call your mother or your father to see how they are," Mrs. Carter said.

"Oh, don't do that!" said Sam.

"Why not?" asked Mrs. Carter.

"They're still in California helping my aunt rebuild her house. It was totally destroyed in the earthquake."

"I see," said Mrs. Carter. She made a mark with her red pencil in her little black book.

Sam knew she had placed the red mark next to his name.

Sam glanced at the clock. School was almost over for the day. He would do his homework tonight, and Mrs. Carter would forget all about his earthquake story.

* * *

That night, having dinner at his dad's house, Sam took large helpings of meat loaf and mashed potatoes. He thought the earthquake story was behind him.

"Have some peas, Sam," his dad said.

Sam took a small spoonful and started eating his meatloaf. Sam was going to dip it into the ketchup when his father said, "I got an interesting phone call today. I hear we were caught in an earthquake in California."

Sam put his fork down.

"Why on earth did you tell Mrs. Carter that lie?" his father asked.

"I don't know," said Sam, looking down at his plate.

"This isn't the first time," his dad said. "You lie a lot, Sam."

"I don't always lie in school," Sam said.

"No," his father agreed. "Sometimes you lie about the strangest things. Like the time you made up the story about that TV program that was never on. Remember the one about the treasure buried in the yard? There was also the time you lied about not crossing the street."

"That was a long time ago! I was six!" Sam shouted.

"But even though you're almost eleven now, you don't seem to have changed," his father replied.

"I try not to lie," Sam said, "but it's hard. It sounds a lot better to say my homework was swallowed up in an earthquake than to tell the truth."

"What was the truth?" his father asked.

"I forgot to do it. But if I said that, Mrs. Carter would think I didn't care."

"What does she think about you when you tell her those earthquake stories?" asked his father.

"Maybe she thinks I have a good imagination?" Sam smiled.

His father shook his head. "I understand it's been hard for you since your mother and I separated. The last six months have been hard for all of us."

"I'm not hurting anyone by lying. My stories are more fun than what's real."

"We live in the real world, Sam," his father said. "People don't like being lied to."

Sam poked at his meat loaf.

"I have an idea," said his father. "I talked to your mother about it and she agreed. Maybe you need some kind of signal for yourself. You can use the signal to stop yourself from lying."

"What do you mean?" Sam asked.

"I'll give you an example," said his father. "When I'm worried about something, I whistle. Whistling helps me to stop worrying so much. It's a way of telling myself to relax. When I remember to whistle, it's a way of helping me break my habit of worrying."

"Do you think that could help me stop lying?" said Sam.

"Sam, do you want to stop lying?" asked his father.

Sam thought for a minute. "I think so."

"What would you like your signal to be?" his father asked.

"I like yours. I could whistle," Sam said. He tried whistling a few notes.

"That sounds good," his father said. "In fact, since we have the same signal, it could be something special between the two of us. It will be our secret."

Sam grinned. "A secret signal," he said. "I like that."

[Chapter 2]

The Dark Green Car

The sun shone brightly at the end of
the school day. Sam and his best friend,
Josh, headed out the door together. Starting
tomorrow they had a long weekend.

"I'll dump my books at my dad's house,
get my bike, and then I'll meet you at the
park," said Sam.

"All right," said Josh. "But your dad's not
home, is he?"

"No, but I've got a key, just in case of emergencies," Sam said.

"Does your dad have anything good to eat?" Josh asked.

"No, he doesn't like treats. All he ever has is fruit and vegetables." Both boys made faces at the thought.

"My mom might have cookies," Josh said.

"My mom never bakes," Sam said. "She's too busy working. But tonight is pizza night."

"Is it hard to live in two different houses?" Josh asked.

"I'm getting used to it," said Sam as he turned toward his dad's house. "See you at the park." It wasn't his night to stay with his dad, but his bike was there and he could stop by later to pick up his books before heading to his mom's house.

In the two weeks since he and his father had talked about his lying, there had been changes. The whistling gave him time to stop and think before he spoke. Still, he was a little sorry to give up his stories.

It had been fun to tell his classmates that he had a pet alligator from Florida. It was fun, that is, until everyone wanted to see it. He had to make up a story about the alligator disappearing. Some kids got angry. They all said he never had a pet. No one wanted to talk to him after that, except Josh. It was great to have a friend who liked him no matter what he did.

As he walked to his father's house, Sam thought about why he lied. He decided it was because his life was so boring. Nothing ever happened to him, nothing exciting anyway. That's just how it was for kids.

Adults did exciting things like fly planes and explore jungles full of dangerous animals. They sailed ships around the world and never had to go to school. Sam wished he were an adult.

Even though his parents were adults, they didn't do anything exciting. His father worked in a lab every day. Sam didn't know exactly what he did there. His mother worked for a doctor. She answered the phone and filled out forms. The doctor wasn't like the ones Sam saw on TV who ran around saving people all the time. Dr. Alexander was a skin doctor. Mostly, he treated teenagers who had pimples and stuff.

Sam knew he'd have an exciting job some day. He could be an animal trainer. That would be fun. Or he could parachute jump from an airplane. Was that a job? If not, it should be.

Sam wanted to be a baseball player, but he wasn't very good at sports. In fact, he wasn't really good at anything, except telling lies. Too bad there wasn't a job like that.

As he neared his dad's house, he dug into his pocket for the key. Before he found it, a man opened the door and stepped outside. Sam had never seen him before. He was tall and thin with black hair. He wore a dark suit and sunglasses. He stood in the doorway and looked up and down the street. He saw Sam, but paid no attention to him. Then the man ducked back into the house.

Sam sat down on the front steps of the neighbors' house. The Brooks lived there. He knew they would be at work. He pretended to tie his shoelace. As he did, he looked up now and then to see what was going on at his dad's house.

The man came back out. A smaller, heavier man was with him. He was bald and wore a gray jacket and brown pants. Sam's heart raced. Who were these people? What were they doing in his house? Should he stay and see what was happening or find a phone and call the police?

A third man came out of the house. The other two stood close by. They began walking. That's when Sam realized the third man was his father.

As they walked down the steps, his father was in the middle. The men walked closely at his sides. They walked toward Sam. He forgot to tie his shoelace.

As his father got closer, Sam opened his mouth to say something. His father saw him and frowned. Before Sam could say anything, his father began whistling.

The tune sounded familiar to Sam. Had he heard it before? Was it a signal for Sam to pretend they didn't know each other?

The men walked to a dark green car parked nearby. Sam reached into his backpack for a pencil and notebook as the tall man got into the driver's seat. The short man sat in the back with his father. His father stared straight ahead.

The driver started the car and it pulled out and sped away. Sam copied the license plate number into his notebook: XRL 5567.

All at once, Sam's life was full of excitement and mystery. He wasn't sure he liked it.

Chapter 3

The Unlocked House

Sam watched the car drive away. Then he ran into the house. Maybe his father had left him a note telling him what was going on.

He started scrambling up the steps but stopped. Maybe there were other people still inside. Sam listened at the door. It sounded quiet. He decided to take a chance and opened the door quickly. It wasn't even locked. What was his father thinking?

Sam looked around and saw the house was a little messy, as if someone were looking for something. There were papers scattered on the kitchen table and some cabinet doors left open. Nothing was obviously wrong, but something was definitely not right.

Sam decided to call his father's work.

"Good afternoon, Dunmore Labs," a woman's voice answered.

"John Dennison, please," Sam said.

"One moment." Sam heard the weird music they always played while he was on hold. Then his father's secretary came on the line.

"Margaret Smithers speaking," she said.

"Hi, Ms. Smithers. It's Sam. Is my dad there?" he asked.

His stomach lurched when he heard her reply.

"I haven't seen him since lunch. He has a business meeting in Boston on Monday and he told me he decided to spend the weekend there," she said.

"He didn't tell me he was going away," Sam said.

"It just came up this morning. He probably told your mother."

"Uh, okay," Sam said. "Did he say where he would be staying in Boston?"

"He's at the Midtown Hotel," she answered. She gave Sam the phone number. Then she added, "But he won't be there yet. I wouldn't call him until later tonight, say around nine p.m. I know he was going out for dinner with some friends."

Sam thanked her and hung up. Then he had a thought. He looked in his father's closet. His overnight suitcase was still there. It seemed as if all of his father's suits were there, too. Sam never looked that closely at what his father wore. Still, the closet seemed pretty full.

What should he do? Was his father in danger? He sat on his father's bed, thinking. Suddenly he remembered Josh was waiting at the park. He locked the door, jumped on his bike, and rode as fast as he could.

Josh was waiting by the big oak tree. "Hey, where have you been? I've been here forever."

"Something bad happened," Sam said. "I saw two strange men come out of my dad's house. My dad was with them and he saw me, but pretended like he didn't know me. He just whistled. Then they all got in a car and drove away."

"So?" Josh asked.

"Whistling is a signal between us," Sam said. "Something's wrong. I know it."

"Come on, let's ride," Josh said.

"Is that all you have to say?" Sam asked. "I think my dad's in danger!"

Josh smiled. "I have to say, this is a good one. It's one of your best stories ever."

"Don't you believe me?" Sam asked. "This one is true. Really."

"Aw, come on. I forgive you for being late," Josh said.

"Cross my heart and hope to die," said Sam. "I'm really not lying."

Josh stared at Sam. "Do you swear this is true?" he asked. "You didn't make this up because you're late?"

"Absolutely," Sam said. "I'm really, really not lying."

"It's hard to believe," Josh said. "Why would your dad go off with those guys? I mean, if he was really in trouble, wouldn't he find a way to tell you what was happening?"

"Maybe he didn't have time," Sam said.

"Who would be after your dad?" asked Josh. "I mean, he's nice and all, but he's not rich or famous, so why would anyone want to take him?"

"I don't know," said Sam.

"Maybe he knows some secret stuff. I was watching this T.V. show and this guy knew something, but he didn't know how important it was. Then the bad guys came and took him away and tried to get him to talk," Josh said.

"What could my dad know?" Sam asked.

"What does he do?" asked Josh.

"He's a computer geek. He works at a lab," Sam said.

"What does he work on?" Josh said. "Maybe it's some kind of important secret formula that would help someone take over the world."

"It's nothing like that," Sam said. "He tries to tell me about it, but it's hard to understand. I don't think it's anything special, really."

"Then I don't see why anyone would want to take him," Josh said. "Let's ride."

As they rode through the park, Sam tried to believe Josh. Why would someone want to kidnap his dad? Was it just his imagination? Adults acted weird most of the time.

Maybe the two men with his dad were just businessmen, boring, stuffy businessmen with serious faces.

"Sam. Hey, Sam!"

Sam realized Josh was talking to him. "I have to go home," Josh said. "Meet me at Scoops after school tomorrow."

Scoops was an ice cream place they liked to hang out in after school. Sam nodded and waved. Then he turned his bike toward his mother's house. Sam thought about his dad again and shivered. He didn't feel like eating ice cream today. His stomach already felt strangely cold.

[Chapter 4]

As Sam pulled up to his mom's house, she was paying a pizza delivery guy.

"Just in time," she said, then frowned. "Where are your books?"

"Oh, I forgot them over at Dad's house," Sam said.

His mother said, "Eat first. Then you can ride your bike over and get them."

As they ate, Sam told his mother what had happened that afternoon.

"There were these creepy men. They were in the house and then they came out with Dad. They made him walk between them. Dad saw me, I swear he saw me. But he didn't say a word. All he did was whistle."

His mother smiled. "You have some imagination, Sam. I'm sure it was just some business people he was meeting with. He probably didn't see you sitting on the neighbors' porch."

"But, Mom, it was too weird. I think Dad's in trouble," Sam said. "I called his office and they said he didn't come back after lunch. They think he left early on a business trip to Boston. I didn't know he was leaving. Did he tell you that he was going away?"

"Yes. He called me to say he might not be back until Thursday, so you're here until then," his mother said. "The trip came up suddenly. That's why he didn't tell you."

"But I looked in his closet and his suitcase was still there. So were most of his clothes," Sam said.

"Sam, you have to stop making up stories," his mother said. "I'm tired of it and you're too old for it. Your father is fine."

"But, Mom," said Sam.

"End of discussion. Help me clean up, then ride over to your father's and get those books," she said.

"I can get them tomorrow morning," Sam said. "I don't have any homework tonight."

"I want you to get them now," his mom said firmly.

It was only fifteen blocks to the house, but the ride seemed endless. When he reached his dad's place, Sam laid his bike at the foot of the steps. He opened the front door and quickly switched on the hall light.

"Dad?" he called. No one answered. He went through the house to his father's bedroom. He turned on the light and opened the closet. The suitcase was still there.

He reached for his backpack when the telephone rang. He knew he should pick it up. But all he wanted to do was get out of the house.

It rang again.

He edged over to the phone and picked it up. There was no one on the other end.

"Hello?" said Sam. Whoever was on the other end of the phone had hung up.

He hiked his backpack over one shoulder, and then the other. He opened the door to leave and the phone rang again.

Someone must be watching the house. He slammed the door behind him.

Sam didn't want to stop to lock it, but knew he should. His fingers kept missing the key. Finally, he twisted it in the lock. He leaped down the steps, grabbed his bike, hopped on, and sped away. In his mind, he could hear the phone still ringing.

He kept looking over his shoulder as he rode. Was someone following him? He couldn't be sure. Streetlights cast shadows against the houses and trees. All he heard was the swish of his tires. Up ahead, he saw the lights from his mom's house.

Sam heard a car coming down the street. It was moving slowly. Sam rode up onto the sidewalk. He was about to bike between two houses when he heard a man's voice. "Hey, kid!" Sam stopped.

"I'm looking for 1520 East Glen Road," the driver said. "Do you know where that is?"

"No," Sam said. "No, I don't."

"Okay, there must be a gas station around here," the man said. "Do you know?"

"I have to go home," Sam said. He took off. He thought he heard the car drive off, but he was pedaling too quickly. At his mom's, he threw his bike down and ran up the front steps.

"Mom!" he yelled. He stood in the open door, panting.

"Sam, what is it now?" said his mom.

"It was really creepy at Dad's house and the phone rang and rang."

"Why didn't you answer it?" his mother said. "I was calling you to make sure you had gotten there okay."

"I didn't know that was you," Sam said. "I guess I was scared."

"I'm sorry if I scared you," his mother said. "How about turning off your imagination long enough to have some ice cream with me." Sam smiled.

They watched TV and ate ice cream, and then Sam got ready for bed.

Lying in the dark, he could hear the sounds of the TV still on. His mother was watching some old show about the Beatles. Sam could hear the old rock music as he put his head down on his pillow.

That's it, he said to himself. The song his father had whistled. It wasn't just any old song. It was a Beatles song.

The name of the song was "Help!"

Chapter 5

Pizza and Problems

It was morning. Sam rubbed his eyes and jumped out of bed. He threw on his clothes and ran down to the kitchen.

His mother was standing by the stove, making oatmeal for breakfast.

"Hey, sleepyhead," she said. "There's juice in the refrigerator."

"Mom, I remembered something important," Sam said.

"What?" his mother asked, slowly stirring the oatmeal.

"That song Dad was whistling," he said. "It was the Beatles song 'Help.'"

"So?"

"It was a signal," Sam said. "It meant that Dad needed help."

His mother pointed the spoon at him. "Sam, I told you last night that I'm tired of this lying business," she said. "I'm sure your father's safe and sound in Boston. I'm not even going to discuss this with you anymore. Now eat."

She spooned the oatmeal into a bowl and sprinkled brown sugar and raisins on top. Sam tried to eat, but he was too upset. He pushed the oatmeal around with his spoon.

"Okay," his mother said. "We'll try to call your father. Where did Ms. Smithers say he was staying?"

Sam smiled.

"The Midtown Hotel." Sam found the crumpled piece of paper where he had written the phone number of the hotel.

"Hello? Hello?" His mother tried talking into the phone.

Sam couldn't understand what was going on. Then she put the phone down. "I can't get through. They say the phone lines are busy," she said. "We'll try again later."

"Okay," Sam said. "Maybe in another ten minutes?" he added hopefully.

"I don't think so," his mother said. "You have to get a move on. I'll meet you at three o'clock right in front of school."

Sam looked at her. What was his mom talking about?

"Don't tell me you forgot. We're going shopping for clothes for you," his mother said. "Remember?"

"I don't need any clothes," said Sam. His heart dropped at the thought. Shopping with his mother was worse than being eaten by cobras. He had only seen one cobra in his life, at the zoo. The huge snake had swallowed a whole chicken in a few minutes.

"Your jeans are full of holes and so are your T-shirts," she said. "Your sneakers have holes in them too. I can't let you run around like that."

"Mom, this is what everybody wears," Sam said.

"Not my son," his mother said. "Now wash up."

"I'm supposed to meet Josh at Scoops," Sam said.

"Call him and tell him you'll meet him later," his mother said. "Now let's get going. I have a lot to do."

"It's okay," Josh said when Sam called him. "Meet me later at the playground. We'll play ball."

The shopping was worse than Sam thought. They went to the mall. Instead of going to cool places like Music World and Computerama, they went to department stores. Sam tried on pants and shirts. His mother insisted he come out to show her each piece of clothing.

At the shoe store, his mom had to look around for someone to help them. When she finally did, Sam wished they could have skipped the shoes altogether.

"Now let's see some shoes that don't cost a fortune," she said. "They're all the same anyway. We don't need some famous athlete's picture on the box."

Sam sunk down in his chair.

Sometimes Sam couldn't understand why his parents had split up. Other times it was easy to see. If he had to go shopping, he wished it was with his dad. At least his dad understood the importance of cool shoes. In his mind, he saw his dad driving away with those strange men, looking straight ahead.

"Sam? Sam!" His mother brought him back to reality. She was showing him a brand of shoes he had never heard of. He slipped his feet into them.

Then he grinned. They were too tight.

"Do you have the next larger size?" his mother asked.

The salesman shook his head.

The next pair was better. They even had a brand name.

"How do they feel?" his mother asked.

Sam walked back and forth. "A lot better," he said.

His mother pinched the end of the sneaker. "They seem roomy enough. Do you like them?"

"You bet," Sam said.

His mother looked at the price.

"We'll take them," she said. She looked at her watch. "I'm hungry. How about you?"

He was starving. At the food court, he got a jumbo hot dog. His mother had a cup of coffee and a muffin.

"Sam, I know this separation has been hard on you," she said.

"But you're taking it better every day," she added. "You don't seem to lie so much. Except for that thing about your dad last night. Anyway, I just want to say I'm really proud of you."

"Thanks, Mom," Sam said.

It felt good to hear her say those things, but Sam couldn't let her know he wasn't giving up on his dad. She would never believe him.

In the middle of the packed food court, Sam felt all alone.

[Chapter 6]

Hard Ball

When they arrived back home, Sam's mom made him hang everything up and even put the new shoes in his closet. He thought it was silly. He was only going to have to take things out again to wear them.

He hurried to change. Sam threw on his oldest jeans and pulled a sweatshirt over his head. Something crinkled as he moved. Sam put his hand in his pocket, hoping that maybe there was a dollar bill in there.

Instead, Sam pulled out a piece of paper. He was just about to throw it away but decided to look at it first. It was the paper he had written the license number on — the license number of the car that the men drove his father away in.

Here was a way to prove to Josh he wasn't lying. He grabbed his tennis ball.

"Bye, Mom," he called on his way out.

"Bye, honey. Be back by six thirty for dinner," she said.

Sam slammed the door and hopped onto his bike. When he got to the playground, Josh was throwing the ball against a wall. Thwack! He threw the ball hard and it bounced back to him. He caught it each time.

"Hey!" he said. "You survived shopping!"

"Just barely," said Sam. "Why do we have to get new clothes anyway?"

"Beats me," said Josh. "I think it's a mom thing."

Sam began throwing his ball like Josh. Thwack!

"Listen, I found something," Sam said.

"What?" Josh asked.

"Remember those guys I told you about? The ones who took my dad?" Sam stopped throwing his ball.

Josh nodded.

"I forgot that I wrote down the license plate number. We could find out who owns the car," Sam said.

"What would that prove?" Josh asked.

"I don't know. But at least I could find out who took him away," said Sam.

"How would you do that?"

"Well, don't you have an aunt or a cousin or someone who works for the license department?" Sam asked.

"It's the Department of Motor Vehicles," Josh said. "My aunt Vi works there." He stopped throwing his ball and shook his head. "You're not getting me and my aunt involved in your crazy stories. No way, Sam!"

"You could just ask her to do you a favor," said Sam.

"I can just hear myself," said Josh. "'Oh, Aunt Vi, could you look up this license plate number and tell me who it belongs to?' She'd want to know why, Sam. What would I say?"

"Please," Sam begged.

"No way. I stood up for you when you told those stories about the alligator and the other stuff, but I'm not doing it this time."

"You've got to stop telling these lies," Josh added. "People would like you a lot better if you did."

"What do you mean?" Sam asked.

"I mean you're a lot of fun," Josh said. He looked uncomfortable. "Just don't tell so many lies. People don't like it."

"What people?" Sam asked.

"Nobody," Josh said. "Forget it."

Sam looked at Josh. "What people?" he asked again.

Josh looked down at his feet. "My parents," he mumbled.

"Who?"

"My parents, okay!" said Josh, looking up at Sam. "They don't like lying. They don't like me hanging around with you because of it."

Sam wanted to yell at Josh.

Sam wanted to say Josh's parents were jerks. His father thought he was a big shot. His mother had mean little eyes. Instead, Sam said, "I'm really worried about my dad. It's not a lie. I'm going to find out where he is and help him. I'll show you that he's really in trouble. If you were really my friend, I wouldn't need to convince you to help me."

Sam turned to go. He got his bike and started to walk it out of the park. Josh came running behind him.

"Look, Sam, I'm sorry," he said. "But you have to admit that you lie a lot."

Sam looked Josh in the eye. "I'm not lying now," he said.

"What are you going to do?" Josh asked.

"I'm going to go over to my dad's house and call the hotel where he's supposed to be staying. If he's there, they'll tell me and I'll know he's okay."

"I'll come with you," Josh said.

They jumped on their bikes and rode out of the park. It was getting late. The trees cast big gloomy shadows on the streets as Josh and Sam rode in silence. Usually, they had races and cheered each other on.

Today they were quiet.

Finally, they got to the house. Sam took out his key and opened the door. He began to walk in. Then he stopped. There were pillows and books on the floor that hadn't been there the last time. The sofa was ripped in the living room. Josh followed Sam as he went into his father's bedroom. The mattress had been torn. Drawers were thrown on the floor.

Josh looked at Sam. "What happened?" he asked, looking around.

"I don't know! It wasn't like this yesterday," Sam answered.

"Do you know the number of the hotel where your dad is staying?" asked Josh.

Sam patted his pockets. "I had it somewhere. I don't know. Never mind. I'll call information."

"Okay, but hurry up. It's creepy in here," Josh said. He looked around at the mess and shivered.

Sam dialed the number of the hotel.

"It's ringing," he said. "Hello. Can I speak to John Dennison? He's a guest in the hotel." He listened for a moment. Then he put the phone back on the hook.

"What did they say?" Josh asked.

Sam looked at Josh. "They said there was no one with that name staying at the hotel."

Chapter 7

A Knock at the Door

"Are you sure?" Josh asked. "You're not just making this up, are you?"

Sam glared at his friend. "Of course not, Josh! I wouldn't fool around about something like this."

"This is getting too scary for me," Josh said. He looked around the room.

"Do you think we should call the police?"

"Maybe," Sam said. He picked up the phone again.

A sharp knock at the door made both of the boys jump.

"Who's that?" whispered Josh.

"I don't know," Sam whispered back.

Slowly the door began to open. The boys scrambled to hide behind the torn sofa. Lying flat on the floor behind the sofa, Sam could hardly catch his breath. He lay there as quietly as he could, staring at Josh.

A woman's voice said, "I thought I heard someone in here." Then there was a gasp. "What on earth?"

Sam peeked over the sofa. It was Mrs. Magruder from next door. She was carrying a bundle of papers in one hand.

"Mrs. Magruder, hi," Sam said as he came out from behind the sofa. "Josh, it's okay."

"What did you do?" Mrs. Magruder asked.

She peered over her thick glasses and pointed to the mess.

"It wasn't us, honest," Sam said. "I came over to get something and we found it like this. We were just going to call the police."

Mrs. Magruder shuffled closer to Sam and looked him in the eye.

"Are you sure you didn't do this, young man?" she asked.

"Why would I want to mess up my own house?" Sam responded.

"Who knows?" she answered, shaking her head. "I just don't understand kids today with their cell phones and their video games. In my day, we were happy to sit quietly and listen to the radio. We'd never dream of making a mess like this."

"We didn't make this mess," Josh said. "What are you doing here anyway?"

Mrs. Magruder looked at Sam and shook her finger at him. "Your father asked me to bring in his newspaper and his mail while he was away. Now, you clean this place up and I won't say anything to your father. You had better not bother the police! They have real crimes to solve, not this silly stuff where you mess up a house. You kids can't fool me!"

She placed the newspaper and the mail on a table and stomped off.

Josh made a face as she closed the door.

"Maybe we shouldn't call the police," Sam said. "She'll tell them that we did this. They'll never believe us."

"You're right. Let's just get out of here," said Josh.

Outside, Sam turned to Josh. "What do we do now?"

"Let me think about it," Josh said, and he rode his bike down the street.

As Sam began to ride away, he thought he saw something move in his dad's backyard. He didn't wait to find out if he was right. He sped down the street toward his mom's house. He wouldn't go back into his dad's house until he knew it was safe.

That night at dinner, Sam wondered what he should tell his mom. Would she think he was lying about the hotel and the mess? By the time they started dessert, he had decided to tell her. Then the phone rang. It was his grandmother. His mother settled in for what would surely be a long talk.

When she finally hung up the phone, he said, "Mom, I called the hotel today where Dad is supposed to be staying," he said.

"Did you talk to him?" his mother asked.

"No, they said they didn't have anyone by that name staying at that hotel," he said.

His mother laughed. "His secretary probably got the hotel name wrong. She was always getting stuff like that wrong. I don't know why your father keeps her on."

"But, Mom, I think there's something wrong," he began to say.

"Don't start that again, Sam. I'm not in the mood, and it's time you go to sleep," his mother said.

She shooed him toward the stairs.

Sam climbed them slowly. His mother didn't believe him. Josh wouldn't help him. Mrs. Magruder thought he had messed up the house. Sam knew there was something wrong. He would just have to find his father by himself — without anybody's help.

Chapter 8

What is Delta Corp?

"Sam!" His mother's voice cut through his dream. Men were chasing him. He kept getting away, but they always caught up. His heart pounded as they reached out for him. He was at a dead end. They were coming to get him.

"Sam! Wake up! Josh is on the phone," his mother yelled.

"What! What!" Sam sat up in bed, his heart still racing.

"Phone!" his mother hollered.

Sam scrambled out of bed and ran down the stairs. His mother held out the phone and he grabbed it.

"Hey!" he said.

"I thought about it last night," said Josh. "I'm going to ask my aunt to trace the license plate. She's working today."

"What made you change your mind?" Sam asked.

"You've never stuck to a lie this long," Josh said. "Of course, if you're lying, I'll never talk to you again. That'll be the end of our friendship."

"I'm not lying," Sam said.

"Come over and we'll call her together," said Josh.

"I'm on my way," Sam said. He hung up and raced up to his room. He threw on his clothes and ran down the stairs.

"Where are you going?" his mother asked. She put her hands on her hips. Sam saw that she was just about to make pancakes, his favorite Saturday breakfast.

"I have to go over to Josh's," Sam said. "It's important."

"What about eating your breakfast?" his mother asked.

"I'll eat over there," Josh said.

"Okay," his mother said. "When are you coming back?"

"Soon," Sam said, and raced out the door. The ride over to Josh's seemed longer than ever. Josh was waiting at the door when Sam got there.

"Come on in," he said.

Josh's mother nodded at Sam as the boys walked into the kitchen. "Hello, Mrs. Trask," said Sam. She walked out of the room, and Sam heard her close a door somewhere.

Josh picked up the phone on the clean kitchen counter.

"I'll put her on speaker so we can both hear her," Josh said. He dialed the number.

"Department of Motor Vehicles," a cheery voice answered.

"Violet Trask, please," Josh said. They listened to some music for a minute and then Josh's aunt came on the phone.

"Hi, Aunt Vi," Josh said.

"Hey, Joshie boy, when are you coming to visit me?" his aunt said.

"Soon," Josh said.

"Good. I've got a new computer game I want to try out with you," his aunt said.

"Aunt Vi, can you trace a license plate number for me?" Josh asked quickly.

"What?" she asked. Her voice had changed from being warm and friendly to something colder. Sam shifted from foot to foot at the sound.

"It's really important," Josh said. "It's for my friend."

"What friend?"

"You know my friend Sam?" Josh asked. "It's a favor for him."

"Is that the boy who lies so much?" his aunt asked. Sam felt as if he had been punched in the stomach.

"He's doing a lot better now," Josh said.

"Glad to hear it. Why does he need to have a license plate traced?" his aunt asked.

"He'll explain it to you," Josh said.

He motioned for Sam to talk into the phone.

Sam felt shy and nervous. How could he explain what had happened to his father? But Aunt Vi was a good listener.

"I don't like this," she said after hearing the story. The phone became silent. Sam knew that Josh's aunt was thinking.

Sam held his breath. Then Aunt Vi's voice came back on the line. "I'll make a deal with you. I'll trace the license plate number, Sam, if you tell your mother what's going on. An adult needs to be involved in this and know what's going on. It sounds pretty serious."

Josh yelled into the phone, "Thanks, Aunt Vi. I owe you."

They listened to more of the music while Aunt Vi traced the license plate. Finally, she came back on the line.

"The car is owned by a company called Delta Corp. The address is 115 Fulton Street."

Chapter 9

What is A.L.I.C.E.?

"So," said Sam, "what are we waiting for?"

Just as they made for the door, the phone rang. Josh picked it up.

"It's for you," he said to Sam. He handed him the phone.

"Hello," Sam said. "No, Mom. I have to go someplace with Josh. I can do my homework tomorrow. We have the day off." He rolled his eyes at Josh. "Do I have to go to Grandma's?"

Sam curled the phone cord around his fingers. "Fine. I'll be home soon."

He hung up. "I have to go home now," Sam said.

Josh walked Sam to the door.

"I could meet you tomorrow afternoon," Sam said. "Can you get out then?"

"Sure," Josh said.

"Meet me at my house and we'll ride downtown," Sam said.

"Okay," Josh said. Sam stepped out onto the steps of Josh's house. The kitchen window was open. He heard Mrs. Trask come into the kitchen, "I don't like you spending so much time with that boy," she said. "He's a liar, Josh. Can't you find some other friends?"

If it weren't for Josh, Sam thought, he wouldn't have any real friends.

Without Josh, Sam would go to school alone and sit alone at lunch and then go home and stay in his room. There would be nothing to look forward to on the weekends.

Sam raced on his bike. He tried to outrun the bad thoughts that kept coming into his head. What if his father was really okay? What if his imagination **had** run away with him? Maybe he was wrong. Maybe his father really was at a meeting in Boston.

Then Sam's common sense took over. He remembered the closet with the suitcase. He remembered the mess at the house. He remembered the hotel with no John Dennison. These were clues. Something must have happened.

He rode home feeling a bit better.

That night after dinner he decided to find out more about his dad's work.

"I know Dad works in a lab," he said to his mother. "But what does he do?"

"It's hard to explain," his mother said. "I hardly understand it myself. I know that it has to do with science."

"Is it important?" Sam asked.

"I think so," his mother said. "It's something called 'artificial intelligence.'"

"What does that mean?" Sam asked.

" 'Artificial' means something fake, something that's not real. You know what 'intelligence' means," his mother said.

"So it's fake intelligence," Sam said. "That doesn't make sense."

"Your father is working on something called 'A-life.' Maybe you should look it up. Try the Internet," his mother suggested. "First clear off the table and load the dishwasher."

Later, Sam sat in front of the computer. It was old and slow. When he finally logged on, he typed in "artificial intelligence." There were lots of articles about it. One part of artificial intelligence seemed to be about making machines act like people.

Sam read about a man who made an artificial duck long ago. The duck could eat, drink, quack, and splash in a pool. It had thousands of moving parts. The article directed him to another on "a-life."

That article said "a-life" was the study of artificial systems that act like natural living systems. He read about machines that could make copies of themselves. One was a computer. Another was an electric toy train.

"Awesome," he thought. "But I wonder what this has to do with Dad?"

Sam read further. He learned there was something called a "chatterbot."

It was a computer robot that could talk. All you had to do was type in your question or statement. The chatterbot would answer you and talk with you. It would have a real conversation with you. That sounded like fun.

Then Sam read something that really scared him.

"Bad chatterbots are made to get people to tell their personal information, like the numbers of their bank accounts, where they live, or the numbers of their credit card accounts."

Maybe the men were trying to get his dad to make a bad chatterbot so they could steal money from people. Sam couldn't figure out how this would work. Then he found a link to a real chatterbot.

It was called A.L.I.C.E.

He typed "Hello Alice" into a box and hit the enter key.

"Hello, unknown human," came back the quick reply.

"Are you a good chatterbot or a bad chatterbot?" Sam asked.

"I do not like to call myself a chatterbot," came back the response.

"What do you call yourself?" Sam asked.

"I like to make new friends," the chatterbot wrote.

"I will be your friend," Sam typed.

"Good. Have you seen any movies?" the chatterbot asked.

Sam described a movie he had seen. The chatterbot seemed to get confused at what Sam was typing. Alice asked a lot of strange questions.

Finally, Sam typed, "I have to do my homework now."

Alice wrote back, "Get busy."

When Sam wrote back and wished the chatterbot a nice day, Alice responded with, "The same to you, unknown human."

Sam thought about the chatterbot. It seemed as if Alice couldn't answer everything.

On the other hand, it had been fun talking with a chatterbot and seeing how it worked. Maybe his dad had found a way to make a better chatterbot. A really good chatterbot could get people to spill important information.

He called Josh. Sam had to tell him what he had found.

"Hey, Josh," he began, "guess what I found!"

Then he stopped. It wasn't Josh's voice on the phone. It was Mrs. Trask.

"Sam?" she asked. "Don't call here at this time of night. Josh is in bed. And you should be too."

She banged the phone down with a crash.

Chapter 10

Who Wants to Know

The next morning dragged on. Sam and his mother were visiting his grandmother. His grandma made eggs and bacon and rolls and muffins. She had even made chocolate cake as a special treat because she knew Sam liked it. He could hardly choke it down.

"What's the matter with you?" his mother asked Sam. "Can't you sit still?"

"I promised Josh I'd meet him," Sam said.

"Josh can wait," his mother said. "How often do you see your grandma?"

Every week, Sam wanted to answer, but he knew he shouldn't. They came here almost every Sunday. Usually, Sam didn't mind. This time, he kept looking at the kitchen clock. Finally, his grandmother said, "Let the boy go, Joan. Friends are really important to a boy his age."

"All right," his mother said. "Be home by six, Sam. It's a school night."

"Okay," Sam said. He kissed them both good-bye. Then he took off.

Josh was waiting outside of Sam's house and looking at his watch.

"Late again," he said. "We have to hurry. I told my folks I'd be home soon."

As they rode downtown, Sam told Josh about what he had found on the Internet.

When Sam described the chatterbot, Josh couldn't wait to try it himself. "It sounds cool," he said. "Maybe your dad was working on something important."

They biked for about half an hour. The buildings they passed were old. Neither boy had been in this part of town before. Finally, Sam saw a sign for Fulton Street. He pointed to it and turned right. Josh followed. They stopped in front of building 115.

"What do we do now?" Josh asked.

"Let's see if anyone's in the building," Sam said, looking around.

The street was quiet. It was Sunday. No one seemed to be around. They walked their bikes to the building.

"Look! It says 'Anston Clock Factory,'" Josh said. He pointed to a faded sign hanging off the side of the building.

"I don't think it's a clock factory anymore," Sam said.

He walked carefully up to the main door. It had a steel sliding door over the entrance. The front windows had bars on them. Sam couldn't see any way in.

Just then a big man came around the side of the building. He looked angry when he saw Sam and Josh.

"What are you kids doing here?" he asked. "You don't belong here. Go home."

"Is this building owned by Delta Corp?" Sam asked. He moved back as the man walked forward.

"Who wants to know?" the man asked. Then Sam realized the man was wearing a uniform. The letters "DC" were sewn on his blue shirt.

Sam pointed to the letters and said, "I guess that answers my question."

"Hey, wise guy, beat it! Get going or you'll be sorry." He began swinging a short club.

Sam could also see something that might have been a gun tucked into the man's belt.

"Okay, we're going," said Josh. He got back on his bike.

"You kids, stay away from here if you know what's good for you!" the man yelled. Then he walked away.

The boys didn't stop until they got to Sam's house. Then they leaned their bikes against the house and began to talk.

"What was that all about?" Josh asked.

"They've got to be hiding something," Sam said. "Otherwise he wouldn't have chased us away like that."

"Something's wrong," he added. "I've got to go back and find out what's going on."

"You really have the guts to go back there?" asked Josh. "That guy was totally scary."

"I'll find a way to hide from him. I've got to get into that building. My dad could be there," Sam said.

He turned to look at his friend.

"I'm going to go tonight," Sam said. "Will you go with me?"

Josh gulped. "I guess so," he said. "I can't let you go alone."

"We'll be careful, I promise." Sam said. "That guy will never see us."

"Okay," said Josh. "I'm going home for dinner. I'll have to say we're going to do some homework together. I'll come over around seven."

Sam cleared the table after dinner and waited for his mom to turn on her favorite TV show. He was getting ready to sneak out when the phone rang.

"Hey, Sam," Josh said.

"Why are you calling?" Sam whispered. "I thought we agreed to meet at my house and ride together."

"There's a problem," Josh said. "My folks won't let me out. My mother's watching my every move. They said I have to do my homework and go to bed early."

"Can't you make up some kind of excuse?" Sam asked.

"They won't buy it," Josh said. "I can't sneak out. My mother's sitting by the door."

"Okay. I'll let you know what happens," Sam said.

"You're going by yourself?" Josh asked.

"I have to," Sam said. "It's my dad. Maybe you can sneak out later."

"Sam, the truth is they don't want me hanging out with you. My mom says you're not a good friend," Josh said.

San felt as if a lump of ice had dropped into his stomach.

"Then I guess I'm in this all alone. Nice knowing you," Sam said.

"Wait!" Josh cried, but Sam had already hung up the phone.

Chapter 11

Whistling in the Dark

It was dark by the time Sam reached the Fulton Street building. There was only one streetlight on the block. A small light glowed above the main door that was still locked behind the steel gate.

Sam hid his bike behind some bushes near the building. There were weeds growing all around the place. The sidewalk was cracked and the building was falling apart. Nobody seemed to be taking care of the building. He wished Josh were with him.

Sam slipped around the side of the building. There were more weeds and some broken glass on the ground. Sam was careful not to step on it. His shoes hardly made a sound as he stepped on packed dirt that bordered the factory.

Sam took a little flashlight out of his pocket. He turned it on. Then he covered the light with his hand. In the little light that escaped, he searched for some way to get into the factory.

He edged around looking for a door or an open window. Then he heard someone breathing hard. He hid in the bushes next to the factory and turned off his flashlight.

A man passed by. Sam could hear him talking to himself. "This is stupid," the man said. "I'm wasting my time here. No one's going to try to get into this dump. I need some coffee to stay awake."

Sam could hardly believe his luck. It was the guard who had scared him off before. Sam waited impatiently in the bushes until he heard the man leave. Then he turned the flashlight back on and slowly moved it up and down the building.

He found what he was looking for. There was a small window open on the ground floor. Sam tried to open it wider, but it was stuck. He strained at it until the window flew up with a screech. Sam listened for signs of the man returning, but it was still quiet.

Sam climbed through the window and into a dark room. There were little scratching sounds. Sam thought maybe he'd found his father. He turned the flashlight on.

The yellow eyes of a large rat stared back at him. Sam moved toward it and the rat ran away. Yuck, he thought.

Slowly, he moved through the room. Everything was silent. He felt nervous, worried. He thought of his dad, and before he knew it, he was whistling "America the Beautiful." Maybe his dad would hear it and know that Sam was here.

Sam whistled as loudly as he could. Then he stopped to listen. He heard a faint whistle reply. It was coming from down the hall. He began running when he suddenly tripped over something.

Sam landed flat on the floor. Dust flew up his nose and he sneezed. He tried to stand up. His foot hurt. He stood up slowly and decided he was okay. Sam pointed his flashlight down to see what he had tripped on. The flashlight didn't work. He had broken it when he fell.

Slowly and carefully, Sam felt his way down the hall. He began whistling again.

Now the answering whistle was sharper and clearer. The sound seemed to be coming from behind a closed metal door. Sam tried to open it, but it wouldn't budge. He shoved against it hard. Then, like the window, the door opened with a screech.

"Dad?" he whispered.

A little light came through the barred windows. Sam could see a dark shape sitting near them. It was his father.

"Dad! Are you all right?" he exclaimed.

"Just tired and hungry," his father said. "Quick, untie me."

It took a while before Sam could untie the ropes around his father. It was hard to see and the ropes were tied tightly. At last his father was free.

"How did you find me?" his father asked.

Sam explained how he and Josh had tracked down the building's address.

"I was so scared when I saw you that day," his father said. "Delta Corp was kidnapping me and I was afraid they'd take you, too. That's why I pretended not to know you. I whistled to give you a clue. I never thought you'd try to rescue me yourself. Where's your mother? Where are the police?"

Sam hung his head. "Nobody would believe me. They thought I was lying again."

His father hugged Sam. "That must have been hard," he said. "We can talk about it later, but we'd better get out of here fast."

"Wait, Dad. Why did they kidnap you? Was it because of artificial intelligence?" Sam asked carefully.

"How do you know about that?" his father replied slowly, looking at Sam.

"I've been reading about it. I even talked to a chatterbot," Sam said.

"That's exactly what they are after. I've been doing experiments to improve the chatterbots. The ones I've been working on could fool you into thinking they were human," his father explained.

"I thought so!" Sam exclaimed. "They wanted to use your experiments to invent one to steal from people. They tore up your house looking for your notes. I guess you wouldn't tell them anything."

"That's right. This is too important to give to crooks," his father said. "Now let's go."

Moving slowly, Sam took his father back down the hall. He was careful to avoid the place where he had tripped before. Finally, they reached the window. Sam found an old chair and helped his father up.

His father made it through the open window and then it was Sam's turn.

"Oof!" Sam flopped on the ground.

"Shh!" His father raised his fingers to his lips. Sam pointed to the bushes and he and his father took cover.

Then Sam heard the sound of the guard coming around the building.

[Chapter 12]

And That's No Lie

The guard never moved far from where Sam and his dad were hiding. Sam's legs cramped and his stomach rumbled. Everything began to hurt.

"When are we going to get out of here?" he whispered to his father.

"He'll have to go to the bathroom sometime," his father whispered back.

The guard looked around as if he had heard something.

Sam bent lower behind the bush. Then a bird flew out of the weeds behind him. Sam nearly cried out. The guard looked at his watch. Then he dialed a number on his cell phone.

"Just another hour or so," he said. "I'll be home soon."

As he talked, the guard paced back and forth. Finally, he hung up. Sam heard the guard unlock a door and step inside.

"Now!" Sam's father said. "Go!"

Sam sped away, but when he looked back, his dad was far behind him. Being tied up for so many days had made him weak and slow.

He motioned to him to hurry up.

Sam waited.

"Don't wait," his father whispered. "Run and get help."

Sam couldn't leave his father alone like this. He stayed with him as his dad ran slowly to the front of the building. It was dark and the small light that burned over the gate didn't help.

"Oof!" Sam ran into somebody in the darkness. The person grabbed him and Sam tried to twist free.

"Sam, it's me!" The person moved away from him.

"Josh?" Sam asked.

"Yeah. I snuck out when my parents went to bed. I couldn't let you do this alone. Is your dad here?" Josh asked.

"Yes," Sam's father said. He came out of the shadows.

"What happened to you, Mr. Dennison?" Josh asked.

"Never mind," he said. "I'll tell you later. Let's just get out of here now."

They walked down the road.

"Where's your bike?" Josh asked Sam.

Sam gasped.

"I left it back near the factory!" he said. "I'll have to go back and get it."

"Leave it," his father said.

"Dad, it's my new bike," Sam said.

"Your safety is more important than any bike. By now, the guard has found out that I'm gone. We have to move quickly," his father said. "Josh, do you have your bike?"

"Yes, Mr. Dennison," Josh replied.

"Ride ahead of us and get the police," Sam's father said. "Sam and I will walk down this road as quickly as we can."

Josh hopped on his bike and took off. Sam hoped the police would hurry. It was creepy walking down the dark road.

Suddenly, his father pulled him into the bushes that grew high beside the road. Whoosh! Sam heard a car pass by.

"That might be the men who kidnapped me," his dad said. "The guard probably found out I was missing and called them."

"What do we do now?" Sam asked.

"We keep moving," his father said.

They walked. Soon Sam heard another car. They dove for the bushes just in time. The car was crawling slowly now.

"Come on out, Dennison. You'll never make it! We can stay here all night. Give us what we want and we'll let you go," a voice from the car called out.

Sam tried to hold his breath. It seemed as if the men could see right through the bushes. At any moment he expected a big hand to clamp onto his shoulder. Then the men would haul them out of the bushes.

Sam stayed as silent as he could, but he knew he was breathing heavily.

Then the car traveled farther down the road. One of the men called out the same message.

They don't know where we are, Sam thought. He breathed a little more easily.

Then another thought struck him. They could stay here all night. The police might not believe Josh. He and his father would be trapped.

They'd be at the mercy of the men from Delta Corp.

"Hang on!" his father whispered.

He felt Sam shaking in the bushes. The car came back. "We know where you are," the man called. "Give it up, Dennison. You must be cold and hungry. It's nice and warm inside the car."

Sam knew they were lying. Still, some part of him wanted to believe them. He was cold. He was hungry.

I won't believe them, he thought to himself. They're liars.

The car stopped. They heard the sound of a door closing. Then they heard footsteps walking their way, coming closer and closer. Sam tried to make himself as small as possible. He knew the man was going to find them. Sam grabbed his father's hand. It was good to be near him.

"What have we here?" the man parted the bushes and looked down at them. Just as he did, Sam heard a loud police siren.

The man stumbled back. He jumped into the car and sped down the road.

"Sam! Mr. Dennison! Where are you?" they heard Josh calling. They stepped out of the bushes and into the light from the beams of a police car.

"Josh! You did it! You got the police to come just in time," Sam said.

"Now what's going on?" asked a tall, brown-haired policeman.

"My dad was kidnapped. They wanted the secrets to making a bad chatterbot. They kept him tied up. I found him and my friend came to help," Sam rushed to say.

"What?" the policeman asked. "I didn't believe it when this kid came in and said we had to rescue you. Now I can't believe what you're saying."

"Is this some story you made up?" asked the officer.

Sam hung his head. No one ever believed him.

Then his father spoke up. "It's all true, officer. You can believe my son."

He put his arm around Sam and pulled him in close.

[About the Author]

Michele Sobel Spirn has written more than fifty books and made seventy videos for children and young adults. She currently teaches creative writing at New York University and the New School University. She holds a B.A. degree from Syracuse University, and an M.F.A. in creative writing from the New School University. Ms. Spirn lives in Brooklyn, New York.

[About the Illustrator]

Niamh O'Connor was born in Ireland and moved to Minnesota as a young child. She graduated from the Minneapolis College of Art and Design with a major in Illustration. O'Connor has illustrated magazine articles and band and concert posters. She says she is "addicted to martial arts" and holds a black belt in Hapkido. She has trained in six different martial art forms and is currently studying Capoeira, a martial art developed in Brazil by African slaves in the 16th Century.

[Glossary]

article (AR-ti-kuhl)—a story published in a magazine or newspaper, or on a Web site

artificial intelligence (ar-ti-FISH-uhl in-TEL-uh-juhnss)—something, such as a computer, that is designed to think and act like a person

chatterbot (CHAT-ur-bot)—a computer program designed to act and talk like a person

Internet (IN-tur-net)—the network that allows millions of computers to connect together

laboratory (LAB-ruh-tor-ee)—a place set up for scientific experiments

trace (TRAYSS)—to find something

[Discussion Questions]

1. Do you think that Sam learned his lesson about lying? Why or why not?

2. Is there any way you can think of that Sam could have convinced his mother he wasn't telling lies about his dad?

3. How did Josh show Sam that he was his friend? Was there ever a time when you thought Josh had given up on Sam?

[Writing Prompts]

1. Think about a time you didn't tell the truth, or when someone lied to you. Write about what happened and how it made you feel.

2. Have you ever been worried about your parents? Write about what happened.

3. Sam had to search for his father by himself. Write about a time when you had to be brave and it felt like you were all on your own.

[Internet Sites]

Do you want to know more about subjects related to this book? Or are you interested in learning about other topics? Then check out FactHound, a fun, easy way to find Internet sites.

Our investigative staff has already sniffed out great sites for you!

Here's how to use FactHound:

1. Visit *www.facthound.com*

2. Select your grade level.

3. To learn more about subjects related to this book, type in the book's ISBN number: **1598890670**.

4. Click the **Fetch It** button.

FactHound will fetch the best Internet sites for you!